ANY KIND OF DOG
by Lynn Reiser
Greenwillow Books, New York
P9-DED-649

Watercolors and a black pen were
used for the full-color art.
The text type is Helvetica Light.

Printed in Singapore
by Tien Wah Press
First Edition

10 9 8 7 6 5 4 3 2 1

Library of Congress
Cataloging-in-Publication Data

Reiser, Lynn.
Any kind of dog / Lynn Reiser.
p. cm.
Summary:
All Richard wants is a dog,
even though his mother
tries to give him other
kinds of pets.
ISBN 0-688-10914-4 (trade)
ISBN 0-688-10915-2 (lib.)
[1. Pets—Fiction.
2. Dogs—Fiction.]
I. Title.
PZ7.R27745An 1992
[E]—dc20
91-12771 CIP AC

for Dick, Chris, and Mort,
who love dogs

Richard wanted a dog, any kind of dog.

But his mother said
a dog was
too much trouble,

so she gave him a caterpillar.

The caterpillar was very nice.
It looked a little like a dog,

but it was not a dog.
Richard wanted a dog.
His mother said
a dog was too much trouble,

so she gave him a mouse.

The mouse was very nice.
It looked a little like a dog,

but it was not a dog.
Richard wanted a dog.
His mother said
a dog was too much trouble,

so she gave him a baby alligator.

The baby alligator was very nice.
It looked a little like a dog,

but it was not a dog.
Richard wanted a dog.
His mother said
a dog was too much trouble,

so she gave him a lamb.

The lamb was very nice.
It looked a little like a dog,

but it was not a dog.
Richard wanted a dog.
His mother said
a dog was too much trouble,

so she gave him a pony.

The pony was very nice.
It looked a little like a dog,

but it was not a dog.
Richard wanted a dog.
His mother said
a dog was too much trouble,

so she gave him a bear.

The bear was very nice.
It looked a little like a dog,

but it was not a dog.

All of the animals were very nice,

but Richard still wanted a dog.

but
it was
worth it.

DOG
CHOW